Sophocles

CW00448496

Philoctetes

Sophocles

Translated by Thomas Francklin

CHARACTERS IN THE PLAY

Ulysses, King of Ithaca
Neoptolemus, son of Achilles
Philoctetes, son of Poeas and Companion of Hercules
A Spy
Hercules
Chorus, composed of the companions of Ulysses and Neoptolemus

[SCENE:— A lonely region on the shore of Lemnos, before a steep cliff in which is the entrance to Philoctetes' cave. Ulysses, Neoptolemus and an attendant enter.]

Ulysses

At length, my noble friend, thou bravest son
Of a brave father — father of us all,
The great Achilles — we have reached the shore
Of sea-girt Lemnos, desert and forlorn,
Where never tread of human step is seen,
Or voice of mortal heard, save his alone,
Poor Philoctetes, Poeas' wretched son,
Whom here I left; for such were my commands
From Grecia's chiefs, when by his fatal wound
Oppressed, his groans and execrations dreadful
Alarmed our hosts, our sacred rites profaned,
And interrupted holy sacrifice.
But why should I repeat the tale? The time
Admits not of delay. We must not linger,
Lest he discover our arrival here,
And all our purposed fraud to draw him hence
Be ineffectual. Lend me then thy aid.
Surveying round thee, canst thou see a rock
With double entrance — to the sun's warm rays
In winter open, and in summer's heat
Giving free passage to the welcome breeze?
A little to the left there is a fountain
Of living water, where, if yet he breathes,
He slakes his thirst. If aught thou seest of this
Inform me; so shall each to each impart
Counsel most fit, and serve our common cause.

Neoptolemus*[leaving Ulysses a little behind him]*

If I mistake not, I behold a cave,
E'en such as thou describst.

Ulysses

Dost thou? which way?

Neoptolemus

Yonder it is; but no path leading thither,
Or trace of human footstep.

Ulysses

In his cell
A chance but he hath lain down to rest:
Look if he hath not.

Neoptolemus*[advancing to the cave]*

Not a creature there.

Ulysses

Nor food, nor mark of household preparation?

Neoptolemus

A rustic bed of scattered leaves.

Ulysses

What more?

Neoptolemus

A wooden bowl, the work of some rude hand,
With a few sticks for fuel.

Ulysses

This is all
His little treasure here.

Neoptolemus

Unhappy man!
Some linen for his wounds.

Ulysses

This must be then
His place of habitation; far from hence
He cannot roam; distempered as he is,

It were impossible. He is but gone
A little way for needful food, or herb
Of power to 'suage and mitigate his pain,
Wherefore despatch this servant to some place
Of observation, whence he may espy
His every motion, lest he rush upon us.
There's not a Grecian whom his soul so much
Could wish to crush beneath him as Ulysses.

[He makes a signal to the Attendant. who retires.]

Neoptolemus

He's gone to guard each avenue; and now,
If thou hast aught of moment to impart
Touching our purpose, say it; I attend.

Ulysses

Son of Achilles, mark me well! Remember,
What we are doing not on strength alone,
Or courage, but oil conduct will depend;
Therefore if aught uncommon be proposed,
Strange to thy ears and adverse to thy nature,
Reflect that 'tis thy duty to comply,
And act conjunctive with me.

Neoptolemus

Well, what is it?

Ulysses

We must deceive this Philoctetes; that
Will be thy task. When he shall ask thee who
And what thou art, Achilles' son reply —
Thus far within the verge of truth, no more.
Add that resentment fired thee to forsake
The Grecian fleet, and seek thy native soil,
Unkindly used by those who long with vows
Had sought thy aid to humble haughty Troy,
And when thou cam'st, ungrateful as they were.
The arms of great Achilles, thy just right,
Gave to Ulysses. Here thy bitter taunts
And sharp invectives liberally bestow
On me. Say what thou wilt, I shall forgive,
And Greece will not forgive thee if thou dost not;

For against Troy thy efforts are all vain
Without his arrows. Safely thou mayst hold
Friendship and converse with him, but I cannot.
Thou wert not with us when the war began,
Nor bound by solemn oath to join our host,
As I was; me he knows, and if he find
That I am with thee, we are both undone.
They must be ours then, these all-conquering arms;
Remember that. I know thy noble nature
Abhors the thought of treachery or fraud.
But what a glorious prize is victory!
Therefore be bold; we will be just hereafter.
Give to deceit and me a little portion
Of one short day, and for thy future life
Be called the holiest, worthiest, best of men.

Neoptolemus

What but to hear alarms my conscious soul,
Son of Laertes, I shall never practise.
I was not born to flatter or betray;
Nor I, nor he — the voice of fame reports —
Who gave me birth. What open arms can do
Behold me prompt to act, but ne'er to fraud
Will I descend. Sure we can more than match
In strength a foe thus lame and impotent.
I came to be a helpmate to thee, not
A base betrayer; and, O king! believe me,
Rather, much rather would I fall by virtue
Than rise by guilt to certain victory.

Ulysses

O noble youth! and worthy of thy sire!
When I like thee was young, like thee of strength
And courage boastful, little did I deem
Of human policy; but long experience
Hath taught me, son, 'tis not the powerful arm,
But soft enchanting tongue that governs all.

Neoptolemus

And thou wouldst have me tell an odious falsehood?

Ulysses

He must be gained by fraud.

Neoptolemus

By fraud? And why
Not by persuasion?

Ulysses

He'll not listen to it;
And force were vainer still.

Neoptolemus

What mighty power
Hath he to boast?

Ulysses

His arrows winged with death
Inevitable.

Neoptolemus

Then it were not safe
E'en to approach him.

Ulysses

No; unless by fraud
He be secured.

Neoptolemus

And thinkst thou 'tis not base
To tell a lie then?

Ulysses

Not if on that lie
Depends our safety.

Neoptolemus

Who shall dare to tell it
Without a blush?

Ulysses

We need not blush at aught
That may promote our interest and success.

Neoptolemus

But where's the interest that should bias me?
Come he or not to Troy, imports it aught
To Neoptolemus?

Ulysses

Troy cannot fall
Without his arrows.

Neoptolemus

Saidst thou not that I
Was destined to destroy her?

Ulysses

Without them
Naught canst thou do, and they without thee nothing.

Neoptolemus

Then I must have them.

Ulysses

When thou hast, remember
A double prize awaits thee.

Neoptolemus

What, Ulysses?

Ulysses

The glorious names of valiant and of wise.

Neoptolemus

Away! I'll do it. Thoughts of guilt or shame
No more appal me.

Ulysses

Wilt thou do it then?
Wilt thou remember what I told thee of?

Neoptolemus

Depend on 't; I have promised — that's sufficient.

Ulysses

Here then remain thou; I must not be seen.
If thou stay long, I'll send a faithful spy,
Who in a sailor's habit well disguised
May pass unknown; of him, from time to time,
What best may suit our purpose thou shalt know.
I'll to the ship. Farewell! and may the god
Who brought us here, the fraudful Mercury,
And great Minerva, guardian of our country,
And ever kind to me, protect us still!

[Ulysses goes out as the Chorus enters. The following lines are chanted responsively between Neoptolemus and the Chorus.]

Chorus

strophe 1 Master, instruct us, strangers as we are,
What we may utter, what we must conceal.
Doubtless the man we seek will entertain
Suspicion of us; how are we to act?
To those alone belongs the art to rule
Who bear the sceptre from the hand of Jove;
To thee of right devolves the power supreme,
From thy great ancestors delivered down;
Speak then, our royal lord, and we obey.

Neoptolemus

systema 1 If you would penetrate yon deep recess
To seek the cave where Philoctetes lies,
Go forward; but remember to return
When the poor wanderer comes this way, prepared
To aid our purpose here if need require.

Chorus

antistrophe 1 O king! we ever meant to fix our eyes
On thee, and wait attentive to thy will;
But, tell us, in what part is he concealed?
'Tis fit we know the place, lest unobserved
He rush upon us. Which way doth it lie?
Seest thou his footsteps leading from the cave,
Or hither bent?

Neoptolemus*[advancing towards the cave]*

systema 2 Behold the double door
Of his poor dwelling, and the flinty bed.

Chorus

And whither is its wretched master gone?

Neoptolemus

Doubtless in search of food, and not far off,
For such his manner is; accustomed here,
So fame reports, to pierce with winged arrows
His savage prey for daily sustenance,
His wound still painful, and no hope of cure.

Chorus

strophe 2 Alas! I pity him. Without a friend,
Without a fellow-sufferer, left alone,
Deprived of all the mutual joys that flow
From sweet society — distempered too!
How can he bear it? O unhappy race
Of mortal man! doomed to an endless round
Of sorrows, and immeasurable woe!

antistrophe 2 Second to none in fair nobility
Was Philoctetes, of illustrious race;
Yet here he lies, from every human aid
Far off removed, in dreadful solitude,
And mingles with the wild and savage herd;
With them in famine and in misery
Consumes his days, and weeps their common fate,
Unheeded, save when babbling echo mourns
In bitterest notes responsive to his woe.

Neoptolemus

systema 3 And yet I wonder not; for if aright
I judge, from angry heaven the sentence came,
And Chrysa was the cruel source of all;
Nor doth this sad disease inflict him still
Incurable, without assenting gods?
For so they have decreed, lest Troy should fall
Beneath his arrows ere the' appointed time
Of its destruction come.

10

Chorus

strophe 3 No more, my son!

Neoptolemus

What sayst thou?

Chorus

Sure I heard a dismal groan
Of some afflicted wretch.

Neoptolemus

Which way?

Chorus

E'en now
I hear it, and the sound as of some step
Slow-moving this way. He is not far from us.
His plaints are louder now.

antistrophe 3 Prepare, my son!

Neoptolemus

For what?

Chorus

New troubles; for behold he comes!
Not like the shepherd with his rural pipe
And cheerful song, but groaning heavily.
Either his wounded foot against some thorn
Hath struck, and pains him sorely, or perchance
He hath espied from far some ship attempting
To enter this inhospitable port,
And hence his cries to save it from destruction.

[Philoctetes enters, clad in rags. He moves with difficulty and is obviously suffering pain from his injured foot.]

Philoctetes

Say, welcome strangers, what disastrous fate
Led you to this inhospitable shore,
Nor haven safe, nor habitation fit

11

Affording ever? Of what clime, what race?
Who are ye? Speak! If I may trust that garb,
Familiar once to me, ye are of Greece,
My much-loved country. Let me hear the sound
Of your long wished-for voices. Do not look
With horror on me, but in kind compassion
Pity a wretch deserted and forlorn
In this sad place. Oh! if ye come as friends,
Speak then, and answer — hold some converse with me,
For this at least from man to man is due.

Neoptolemus

Know, stranger, first what most thou seemst to wish;
We are of Greece.

Philoctetes

Oh! happiness to hear!
After so many years of dreadful silence,
How welcome was that sound! Oh! tell me, son,
What chance, what purpose, who conducted thee?
What brought thee thither, what propitious gale?
Who art thou? Tell me all — inform me quickly.

Neoptolemus

Native of Scyros, hither I return;
My name is Neoptolemus, the son
Of brave Achilles. I have told thee all.

Philoctetes

Dear is thy country, and thy father dear
To me, thou darling of old Lycomede;
But tell me in what fleet, and whence thou cam'st.

Neoptolemus

From Troy.

Philoctetes

From Troy? I think thou wert not with us
When first our fleet sailed forth.

Neoptolemus

Wert thou then there?
Or knowst thou aught of that great enterprise?

Philoctetes

Know you not then the man whom you behold?

Neoptolemus

How should I know whom I had never seen?

Philoctetes

Have you ne'er heard of me, nor of my name?
Hath my sad story never reached your ear?

Neoptolemus

Never.

Philoctetes

Alas! how hateful to the gods,
How very poor a wretch must I be then,
That Greece should never hear of woes like mine!
But they who sent me hither, they concealed them,
And smile triumphant, whilst my cruel wounds
Grow deeper still. O, sprung from great Achilles!
Behold before thee Poeas' wretched son,
With whom, a chance but thou hast heard, remain
The dreadful arrows of renowned Alcides,
E'en the unhappy Philoctetes — him
Whom the Atreidae and the vile Ulysses
Inhuman left, distempered as I was
By the envenomed serpent's deep-felt wound.
Soon as they saw that, with long toil oppressed,
Sleep had o'ertaken me on the hollow rock,
There did they leave me when from Chrysa's shore
They bent their fatal course; a little food
And these few rags were all they would bestow.
Such one day be their fate! Alas! my son,
How dreadful, thinkst thou, was that waking to me,
When from my sleep I rose and saw them not!
How did I weep! and mourn my wretched state!
When not a ship remained of all the fleet
That brought me here — no kind companion left
13

To minister or needful food or balm
To my sad wounds. On every side I looked,
And nothing saw but woe; of that indeed
Measure too full. For day succeeded day,
And still no comfort came; myself alone
Could to myself the means of life afford,
In this poor grotto. On my bow I lived:
The winged dove, which my sharp arrow slew,
With pain I brought into my little hut,
And feasted there; then from the broken ice
I slaked my thirst, or crept into the wood
For useful fuel; from the stricken flint
I drew the latent spark, that warms me still
And still revives. This with my humble roof
Preserve me, son. But, oh! my wounds remain.
Thou seest an island desolate and waste;
No friendly port nor hopes of gain to tempt,
Nor host to welcome in the traveller;
Few seek the wild inhospitable shore.
By adverse winds, sometimes th' unwilling guests,
As well thou mayst suppose, were hither driven;
But when they came, they only pitied me,
Gave me a little food, or better garb
To shield me from the cold; in vain I prayed
That they would bear me to my native soil,
For none would listen. Here for ten long years
Have I remained, whilst misery and famine
Keep fresh my wounds, and double my misfortune.
This have th' Atreidae and Ulysses done,
And may the gods with equal woes repay them!

Leader of the Chorus

O, son of Poeas! well might those, who came
And saw thee thus, in kind compassion weep;
I too must pity thee — I can no more.

Neoptolemus

I can bear witness to thee, for I know
By sad experience what th' Atreidae are,
And what Ulysses.

Philoctetes

Hast thou suffered then?
And dost thou hate them too?

Neoptolemus

Oh! that these hands
Could vindicate my wrongs! Mycenae then
And Sparta should confess that Scyros boasts
Of sons as brave and valiant as their own.

Philoctetes

O noble youth! But wherefore cam'st thou hither?
Whence this resentment?

Neoptolemus

I will tell thee all,
If I can bear to tell it. Know then, soon
As great Achilles died —

Philoctetes

Oh, stay, my son!
Is then Achilles dead?

Neoptolemus

He is, and not
By mortal hand, but by Apollo's shaft
Fell glorious.

Philoctetes

Oh! most worthy of each other,
The slayer and the slain! Permit me, son,
To mourn his fate, ere I attend to thine.

Neoptolemus

Alas! thou needst not weep for others' woes,
Thou hast enough already of thy own.

Philoctetes

'Tis very true; and therefore to thy tale.

Neoptolemus

Thus then it was. Soon as Achilles died,
Phoenix, the guardian of his tender years,
Instant sailed forth, and sought me out at Scyros;
With him the wary chief Ulysses came.
They told me then (or true or false I know not),
My father dead, by me, and me alone
Proud Troy must fall. I yielded to their prayers;
I hoped to see at least the dear remains
Of him whom living I had long in vain
Wished to behold. Safe at Sigeum's port
Soon we arrived. In crowds the numerous host
Thronged to embrace me, called the gods to witness
In me once more they saw their loved Achilles
To life restored; but he, alas! was gone.
I shed the duteous tear, then sought my friends
Th' Atreidae friends I thought 'em!-claimed the arms
Of my dead father, and what else remained
His late possession: when — O cruel words!
And wretched I to hear them — thus they answered:
"Son of Achilles, thou in vain demandst
Those arms already to Ulysses given;
The rest be thine." I wept. "And is it thus,"
Indignant I replied, "ye dare to give
My right away?" "Know, boy," Ulysses cried,
"That right was mine. and therefore they bestowed
The boon on me: me who preserved the arms,
And him who bore them too." With anger fired
At this proud speech, I threatened all that rage
Could dictate to me if he not returned them.
Stung with my words, yet calm, he answered me:
"Thou wert not with us; thou wert in a place
Where thou shouldst not have been; and since thou meanst
To brave us thus, know, thou shalt never bear
Those arms with thee to Scyros; 'tis resolved."
Thus injured, thus deprived of all I held
Most precious, by the worst of men, I left
The hateful place, and seek my native soil.
Nor do I blame so much the proud Ulysses
As his base masters — army, city, all
Depend on those who rule. When men grow vile
The guilt is theirs who taught them to be wicked.

I've told thee all, and him who hates the Atreidae
I hold a friend to me and to the gods.

Chorus[*singing*]

O Earth! thou mother of great Jove,
Embracing all with universal love,
Author benign of every good,
Through whom Pactolus rolls his golden flood!
To thee, whom in thy rapid car
Fierce lions draw, I rose and made my prayer —
To thee I made my sorrows known,
When from Achilles' injured son
Th' Atreidae gave the prize, that fatal day
When proud Ulysses bore his arms away.

Philoctetes

I wonder not, my friend, to see you here,
And I believe the tale; for well I know
The man who wronged you, know the base Ulysses
Falsehood and fraud dwell on his lips, and nought
That's just or good can be expected from him.
But strange it is to me that, Ajax present,
He dare attempt it.

Neoptolemus

Ajax is no more;
Had he been living, I had ne'er been spoiled
Thus of my right.

Philoctetes

Is he then dead?

Neoptolemus

He is.

Philoctetes

Alas! the son of Tydeus, and that slave,
Sold by his father Sisyphus, they live,
Unworthy as they are.

Neoptolemus

Alas! they do,
And flourish still.

Philoctetes

My old and worthy friend
The Pylian sage, how is he? He could see
Their arts, and would have given them better counsels.

Neoptolemus

Weighed down with grief he lives, but most unhappy,
Weeps his lost son, his dear Antilochus.

Philoctetes

O double woe! whom I could most have wished
To live and to be happy, those to perish!
Ulysses to survive! It should not be.

Neoptolemus

Oh! 'tis a subtle foe; but deepest plans
May sometimes fail.

Philoctetes

Where was Patroclus then,
Thy father's dearest friend?

Neoptolemus

He too was dead.
In war, alas — so fate ordains it ever —
The coward 'scapes, the brave and virtuous fall.

Philoctetes

It is too true; and now thou talkst of cowards,
Where is that worthless wretch, of readiest tongue,
Subtle and voluble?

Neoptolemus

Ulysses?

Philoctetes

No;
Thersites, ever talking, never heard.

Neoptolemus

I have not seen him, but I hear he lives.

Philoctetes

I did not doubt it: evil never dies;
The gods take care of that. If aught there be
Fraudful and vile, 'tis safe; the good and just
Perish unpitied by them. Wherefore is it?
When gods do ill, why should we worship them?

Neoptolemus

Since thus it is, since virtue is oppressed,
And vice triumphant, who deserve to live
Are doomed to perish, and the guilty reign.
Henceforth, O son of Poeas! far from Troy
And the Atreidae will I live remote.
I would not see the man I cannot love.
My barren Scyros shall afford me refuge,
And home — felt joys delight my future days.
So, fare thee well, and may th' indulgent gods
Heal thy sad wound, and grant thee every wish
Thy soul can form! Once more, farewell! I go,
The first propitious gale.

Philoctetes

What! now, my son?
So soon?

Neoptolemus

Immediately; the time demands
We should be near, and ready to depart.

Philoctetes

Now, by the memory of thy honoured sire,
By thy loved mother, by whate'er remains
On earth most dear to thee, oh! hear me now,
Thy suppliant! Do not, do not thus forsake me,

Alone, oppressed, deserted, as thou seest,
In this sad place. I shall, I know it must, be
A burthen to thee. But, oh! bear it kindly;
For ever doth the noble mind abhor
Th' ungenerous deed, and loves humanity;
Disgrace attends thee if thou dost forsake me,
If not, immortal fame rewards thy goodness.
Thou mayst convey me safe to Oeta's shores
In one short day; I'll trouble you no longer.
Hide me in any part where I may least
Molest you. Hear me! By the guardian god
Of the poor suppliant, all — protecting Jove,
I beg. Behold me at thy feet, infirm,
And wretched as I am, I clasp thy knees.
Leave me not here then, where there is no mark
Of human footstep — take me to thy home!
Or to Euboea's port, to Oeta, thence
Short is the way to Trachin, or the banks
Of Spercheius' gentle stream, to meet my father,
If yet he lives; for, oh! I begged him oft
By those who hither came, to fetch me hence —
Or is he dead, or they neglectful bent
Their hasty course to their own native soil.
Be thou my better guide! Pity and save
The poor and wretched. Think, my son, how frail
And full of danger is the state of man —
Now prosperous, now adverse. Who feels no ills
Should therefore fear them; and when fortune smiles
Be doubly cautious, lest destruction come
Remorseless on him, and he fall unpitied.

Chorus[*singing*]

Oh, pity him, my lord, for bitterest woes
And trials most severe he hath recounted;
Far be such sad distress from those I love!
Oh! if thou hat'st the base Atreidae, now
Revenge thee on them, serve their deadliest foe;
Bear the poor suppliant to his native soil;
So shalt thou bless thy friend, and 'scape the wrath
Of the just gods, who still protect the wretched.

Neoptolemus

Your proffered kindness, friends, may cost you dear;
When you shall feel his dreadful malady
Oppress you sore, you will repent it.

Leader of the Chorus

Never
Shall that reproach be ours.

Neoptolemus

In generous pity
Of the afflicted thus to be o'ercome
Were most disgraceful to me; he shall go.
May the kind gods speed our departure hence,
And guide our vessels to the wished-for shore!

Philoctetes

O happy hour! O kindest, best of men!
And you my dearest friends! how shall I thank you?
What shall I do to show my grateful heart?
Let us be gone! But, oh! permit me first
To take a last farewell of my poor hut,
Where I so long have lived. Perhaps you'll say
I must have had a noble mind to bear it.
The very sight to any eyes but mine
Were horrible, but sad necessity
At length prevailed, and made it pleasing to me.

Leader

One from our ship, my lord, and with him comes
A stranger. Stop a moment till we hear
Their business with us.

[The Spy enters, dressed as a merchant. He is accompanied by one of
Neoptolemus'men.]

Spy

Son of great Achilles,
Know, chance alone hath brought me hither, driven
By adverse winds to where thy vessels lay,
As home I sailed from Troy. There did I meet
This my companion, who informed me where

Thou mightst be found. Hence to pursue my course
And not to tell thee what concerns thee near
Had been ungenerous, thou perhaps meantime
Of Greece and of her counsels naught suspecting,
Counsels against thee not by threats alone
Or words enforced, but now in execution.

Neoptolemus

Now by my virtue, stranger, for thy news
I am much bound to thee, and will repay
Thy service. Tell me what the Greeks have done.

Spy

A fleet already sails to fetch thee back,
Conducted by old Phoenix, and the sons
Of valiant Theseus.

Neoptolemus

Come they then to force me?
Or am I to be won by their persuasion?

Spy

I know not that; you have what I could learn.

Neoptolemus

And did the' Atreidae send them?

Spy

Sent they are,
And will be with you soon.

Neoptolemus

But wherefore then
Came not Ulysses? Did his courage fail?

Spy

He, ere I left the camp, with Diomede
On some important embassy sailed forth
In search —

Neoptolemus

Of whom?

Spy

There was a man — but stay,
Who is thy friend here, tell me, but speak softly.

Neoptolemus*[whispering to him]*

The famous Philoctetes.

Spy

Ha! begone then!
Ask me no more — away, immediately!

Philoctetes

What do these dark mysterious whispers mean?
Concern they me, my son?

Neoptolemus

I know not what
He means to say, but I would have him speak
Boldly before us all, whate'er it be.

Spy

Do not betray me to the Grecian host,
Nor make me speak what I would fain conceal.
I am but poor — they have befriended me.

Neoptolemus

In me thou seest an enemy confest
To the Atreidae. This is my best friend
Because he hates them too; if thou art mine,
Hide nothing then.

Spy

Consider first.

Neoptolemus

I have.

Spy

The blame will be on you.

Neoptolemus

Why, let it be:
But speak, I charge thee.

Spy

Since I must then, know,
In solemn league combined, the bold Ulysses
And gallant Diomede have sworn by force
Or by persuasion to bring back thy friend:
The Grecians heard Laertes' son declare
His purpose; far more resolute he seemed
Than Diomede, and surer of success.

Neoptolemus

But why the' Atreidae, after so long time,
Again should wish to see this wretched exile,
Whence this desire? Came it from th' angry gods
To punish thus their inhumanity?

Spy

I can inform you; for perhaps from Greece
Of late you have not heard. There was a prophet,
Son of old Priam, Helenus by name,
Hlim, in his midnight walks, the wily chief
Ulysses, curse of every tongue, espied;
Took him. and led him captive. to the Creeks
A welcome spoil. Much he foretold to all,
And added last that Troy should never fall
Till Philoctetes from this isle returned.
Ulysses heard, and instant promise gave
To fetch him hence; he hoped by gentle means
To gain him; those successless, force at last
Could but compel him. He would go, he cried,
And if he failed his head should pay th' forfeit.
I've told thee all, and warn thee to be gone,
Thou and thy friend, if thou wouldst wish to save him.

Philoctetes

And does the traitor think he can persuade me?
As well might he persuade me to return
From death to life, as his base father did.

Spy

Of that know not: I must to my ship.
Farewell, and may the gods protect you both!

[The Spy departs.]

Philoctetes

Lead me — expose me to the Grecian host!
And could the insolent Ulysses hope
With his soft flatteries e'er to conquer me?
No! Sooner would I listen to the voice
Of that fell serpent, whose envenomed tongue
Hath lamed me thus. But what is there he dare not
Or say or do? I know he will be here
E'en now, depend on't. Therefore, let's away!
Quick let the sea divide us from Ulysses.
Let us be gone; for well-timed expedition,
The task performed, brings safety and repose.

Neoptolemus

Soon as the wind permits us we embark,
But now 'tis adverse.

Philoctetes

Every wind is fair
When we are flying from misfortune.

Neoptolemus

True;
And 'tis against them too.

Philoctetes

Alas! no storms
Can drive back fraud and rapine from their prey.

Neoptolemus

I'm ready. Take what may be necessary,
And follow me.

Philoctetes

I want not much.

Neoptolemus

Perhaps
My ship will furnish you.

Philoctetes

There is a plant
Which to my wound gives some relief; I must
Have that.

Neoptolemus

Is there aught else?

Philoctetes

Alas! my bow
I had forgot. I must not lose that treasure.

[Philoctetes steps into the cave, and brings out his bow and arrows.]

Neoptolemus

Are these the famous arrows then?

Philoctetes

They are.

Neoptolemus

And may I be permitted to behold,
To touch, to pay my adoration to them?

Philoctetes

In these, my son, in everything that's mine
Thou hast a right,

Neoptolemus

But if it be a crime,
I would not; otherwise —

Philoctetes

Oh! thou art full
Of piety; in thee it is no crime;
In thee, my friend, by whom alone I look
Once more with pleasure on the radiant sun —
By whom I live — who giv'st me to return
To my dear father, to my friends, my country:
Sunk as I was beneath my foes, once more
I rise to triumph o'er them by thy aid:
Behold them, touch them, but return them to me,
And boast that virtue which on thee alone
Bestowed such honour. Virtue made them mine.
I can deny thee nothing: he, whose heart
Is grateful can alone deserve the name
Of friend, to every treasure far superior.

Neoptolemus

Go in.

Philoctetes

Come with me; for my painful wound
Requires thy friendly hand to help me onward.

[They go into the cave.]

Chorus[singing]

strophe 1 Since proud Ixion, doomed to feel
The tortures of th' eternal wheel,
Bound by the hand of angry Jove,
Received the due rewards of impious love;
Ne'er was distress so deep or woe so great
As on the wretched Philoctetes wait;
Who ever with the just and good,
Guiltless of fraud and rapine, stood,
And the fair paths of virtue still pursued;
Alone on this inhospitable shore,
Where waves for ever beat and tempests roar,
How could he e'er or hope or comfort know,

27

Or painful life support beneath such weight of woe?

antistrophe 1 Exposed to the inclement skies,
Deserted and forlorn he lies,
No friend or fellow-mourner there
To soothe his sorrows and divide his care,
Or seek the healing plant of power to 'suage
His aching wound and mitigate its rage;
But if perchance, awhile released
From torturing pain, he sinks to rest,
Awakened soon, and by sharp hunger prest,
Compelled to wander forth in search of food,
He crawls in anguish to the neighbouring wood;
Even as the tottering infant in despair
Who mourns an absent mother's kind supporting care.

strophe 2 The teeming earth, who mortals still supplies
With every good, to him her seed denies;
A stranger to the joy that flows
From the kind aid which man on man bestows;
Nor food, alas! to him was given,
Save when his arrows pierced the birds of heaven;
Nor e'er did Bacchus' heart-expanding bow!
For ten long years relieve his cheerless soul;
But glad was he his eager thirst to slake
In the unwholesome pool, or ever-stagnant lake.

antistrophe 2 But now, behold the joyful captive freed;
A fairer fate, and brighter days succeed:
For he at last hath found a friend
Of noblest race, to save and to defend,
To guide him with protecting hand,
And safe restore him to his native land;
On Spercheius' flowery banks to join the throng
Of Malian nymphs, and lead the choral song
On Oeta's top, which saw Alcides rise,
And from the flaming pile ascend his native skies.

[Neoptolemus and Philoctetes enter from the cave. Philoctetes is suddenly seized with spasms of pain. He still holds in his hand the bow and arrows.]

Neoptolemus

Come, Philoctetes; why thus silent? Wherefore
This sudden terror on thee?

Philoctetes

Oh!

Neoptolemus

Whence is it?

Philoctetes

Nothing, my son; go on!

Neoptolemus

Is it thy wound
That pains thee thus?

Philoctetes

No; I am better now.
O gods!

Neoptolemus

Why dost thou call thus on the gods?

Philoctetes

To smile propitious, and preserve us — Oh!

Neoptolemus

Thou art in misery. Tell me — wilt thou not?
What is it?

Philoctetes

O my son! I can no longer
Conceal it from thee. Oh! I die, I perish;
By the great gods let me implore thee, now
This moment, if thou hast a sword. oh! strike,
Cut off this painful limb, and end my being!

Neoptolemus

What can this mean, that unexpected thus
It should torment thee?

Philoctetes

Know you not, my son?

Neoptolemus

What is the cause?

Philoctetes

Can you not guess it?

Neoptolemus

No.

Philoctetes

Nor I.

Neoptolemus

That's stranger still.

Philoctetes

My son, my son

Neoptolemus

This new attack is terrible indeed!

Philoctetes

'Tis inexpressible! Have pity on me!

Neoptolemus

What shall I do?

Philoctetes

Do not be terrified,
And leave me. Its returns are regular,
And like the traveller, when its appetite
Is satisfied, it will depart. Oh! oh!

Neoptolemus

Thou art oppressed with ills on every side.
Give me thy hand. Come, wilt thou lean upon me?

Philoctetes

No; but these arrows take; preserve 'em for me.
A little while, till I grow better. Sleep

Is coming on me, and my pains will cease.
Let me be quiet. If meantime our foes
Surprise thee, let nor force nor artifice
Deprive thee of the great, the precious trust
I have reposed in thee; that were ruin
To thee, and to thy friend.

Neoptolemus

Be not afraid —
No hands but mine shall touch them; give them to me.

Philoctetes

Receive them, son; and let it be thy prayer
They bring not woes on thee, as they have done
To me and to Alcides.

[Philoctetes gives him the bow and arrows.]

Neoptolemus

May the gods
Forbid it ever! May they guide our course
And speed our prosperous sails!

Philoctetes

Alas! my son,
I fear thy vows are vain. Behold my blood
Flows from the wound? Oh how it pains me! Now
It comes, it hastens! Do not, do not leave me!
Oh! that Ulysses felt this racking torture,
E'en to his inmost soul! Again it comes!
O Agamemnon! Menelaus! why
Should not you bear these pangs as I have done?
O death! where art thou, death? so often called,
Wilt thou not listen? wilt thou never come?
Take thou the Lemnian fire, my generous friend,
Do me the same kind office which I did
For my Alcides. These are thy reward;
He gave them to me. Thou alone deservest
The great inheritance. What says my friend?
What says my dear preserver? Oh! where art thou?

Neoptolemus

I mourn thy hapless fate.

Philoctetes

Be of good cheer,
Quick my disorder comes, and goes as soon;
I only beg thee not to leave me here.

Neoptolemus

Depend on 't, I will stay.

Philoctetes

Wilt thou indeed?

Neoptolemus

Trust me, I will.

Philoctetes

I need not bind thee to it
By oath.

Neoptolemus

Oh, no! 'twere impious to forsake thee.

Philoctetes

Give me thy hand, and pledge thy faith.

Neoptolemus

I do.

Philoctetes*[pointing up to heaven]*

Thither, oh, thither lead!

Neoptolemus

What sayst thou? where?

Philoctetes

Above —

Neoptolemus

What, lost again? Why lookst thou thus
On that bright circle?

Philoctetes

Let me, let me go!

Neoptolemus[*lays hold of him*]

Where wouldst thou go?

Philoctetes

Loose me.

Neoptolemus

I will not.

Philoctetes

Oh!
You'll kill me, if you do not.

Neoptolemus[*lets him go*]

There, then; now
Is thy mind better?

Philoctetes

Oh! receive me, earth!
Receive a dying man. Here must I lie;
For, oh! my pain's so great I cannot rise.

[*Philoctetes sinks down on the earth near the entrance of the cave.*]

Neoptolemus

Sleep hath o'ertaken him. See, his head is lain
On the cold earth; the balmy sweat thick drops
From every limb, and from the broken vein
Flows the warm blood; let us indulge his slumbers.

Chorus[*singing*]

Sleep, thou patron of mankind,
Great physician of the mind,
Who dost nor pain nor sorrow know,
Sweetest balm of every woe,
Mildest sovereign, hear us now;
Hear thy wretched suppliant's vow;
His eyes in gentle slumbers close,

And continue his repose;
Hear thy wretched suppliant's vow,
Great physician, hear us now.
And now, my son, what best may suit thy purpose
Consider well, and how we are to act.
What more can we expect? The time is come;
For better far is opportunity
Seized at the lucky hour than all the counsels
Which wisdom dictates or which craft inspires.

Neoptolemus*[chanting]*

He hears us not. But easy as it is
To gain the prize, it would avail us nothing
Were he not with us. Phoebus hath reserved
For him alone the crown of victory;
But thus to boast of what we could not do,
And break our word, were most disgraceful to us.

Chorus*[singing]*

The gods will guide us, fear it not, my son;
But what thou sayst speak soft, for well thou knowst
The sick man's sleep is short. He may awake
And hear us; therefore let us hide our purpose.
If then thou thinkst as he does — thou knowst whom —
This is the hour. At such a time, my son,
The wisest err. But mark me, the wind's fair,
And Philoctetes sleeps, void of all help —
Lame, impotent, unable to resist,
He is as one among the dead. E'en now
We'll take him with us. 'Twere an easy task.
Leave it to me, my son. There is no danger.

Neoptolemus

No more! His eyes are open. See, he moves.

Philoctetes*[awaking]*

O fair returning light! beyond my hope;
You too, my kind preservers! O my son!
I could not think thou wouldst have stayed so long
In kind compassion to thy friend. Alas!
The Atreidae never would have acted thus.
But noble is thy nature, and thy birth,
And therefore little did my wretchedness,

34

Nor from my wounds the noisome stench deter
Thy generous heart. I have a little respite;
Help me, my son I I'll try to rise; this weakness
Will leave me soon, and then we'll go together.

Neoptolemus

I little thought to find thee thus restored.
Trust me, I joy to see thee free from pain,
And hear thee speak; the marks of death were on thee,
Raise thyself up; thy friends here, if thou wilt,
Shall carry thee, 'twill be no burthen to them
If we request it.

Philoctetes

No; thy hand alone;
I will not trouble them; 'twill be enough
If they can bear with me and my distemper
When we embark.

Neoptolemus

Well, be it so; but rise.

Philoctetes*[rising]*

Oh I never fear; I'll rise as well as ever.

Neoptolemus*[half to himself]*

How shall I act?

Philoctetes

What says my son?

Neoptolemus

Alas!
I know not what to say; my doubtful mind —

Philoctetes

Talked you of doubts? You did not surely.

Neoptolemus

Aye,
That's my misfortune.

Philoctetes

Is then my distress
The cause at last you will not take me with you?

Neoptolemus

All is distress and misery when we act
Against our nature and consent to ill.

Philoctetes

But sure to help a good man in misfortunes
Is not against thy nature.

Neoptolemus

Men will call me
A villain; that distracts me.

Philoctetes

Not for this;
For what thou meanst to do thou mayst deserve it

Neoptolemus

What shall I do? Direct me, Jove! To hide
What I should speak, and tell a base untruth
Were double guilt.

Philoctetes

He purposes at last,
I fear it much, to leave me.

Neoptolemus

Leave thee! No!
But how to make thee go with pleasure hence,
There I'm distressed.

Philoctetes

I understand thee not;
What means my son?

Neoptolemus

I can no longer hide
The dreadful secret from thee; thou art going
To Troy, e'en to the Greeks, to the Atreidae.

Philoctetes

Alas! what sayest thou?

Neoptolemus

Do not weep, but hear me.

Philoctetes

What must I hear? what wilt thou do with me?

Neoptolemus

First set thee free; then carry thee, my friend,
To conquer Troy.

Philoctetes

Is this indeed thy purpose?

Neoptolemus

This am I bound to do.

Philoctetes

Then am I lost,
Undone, betrayed. Canst thou, my friend, do this?
Give me my arms again.

Neoptolemus

It cannot be.
I must obey the powers who sent me hither;
justice enjoins — the common cause demands it,

Philoctetes

Thou worst of men, thou vile artificer
Of fraud most infamous, what hast thou done?
How have I been deceived? Dost thou not blush
To look upon me, to behold me thus
Beneath thy feet imploring? Base betrayer!

To rob me of my bow, the means of life,
The only means — give 'em, restore 'em to me!
Do not take all Alas Alas! he hears me not,
Nor deigns to speak, but casts an angry look
That says I never shall be free again.
O mountains, rivers, rocks, and savage herds!
To you I speak — to you alone I now
Must breathe my sorrows; you are wont to hear
My sad complaints, and I will tell you all
That I have suffered from Achilles' son,
Who, bound by solemn oath to bear me hence
To my dear native soil, now sails for Troy.
The perjured wretch first gave his plighted hand,
Then stole the sacred arrows of my friend,
The son of Jove, the great Alcides; those
He means to show the Greeks, to snatch me hence
And boast his prize, as if poor Philoctetes,
This empty shade, were worthy of his arm.
Had I been what I was, he ne'er had thus
Subdued me, and e'en now to fraud alone
He owes the conquest. I have been betrayed!
Give me my arms again, and be thyself
Once more. Oh, speak! Thou wilt not? Then I'm lost.
O my poor hut! again I come to thee
Naked and destitute of food; once more
Receive me, here to die; for now, no longer
Shall my swift arrow reach the flying prey,
Or on the mountains pierce the wandering herd:
I shall myself afford a banquet now
To those I used to feed on — they the hunters,
And I their easy prey; so shall the blood
Which I so oft have shed be paid by mine;
And all this too from him whom once I deemed
Stranger to fraud nor capable of ill;
And yet I will not curse thee till I know
Whether thou still retainst thy horrid purpose,
Or dost repent thee of it; if thou dost not,
Destruction wait thee!

Leader of the Chorus

We attend your pleasure,
My royal lord, we must be gone; determine
To leave, or take him with us.

Neoptolemus

His distress
Doth move me much. Trust me, I long have felt
Compassion for him.

Philoctetes

Oh then by the gods
Pity me now, my son, nor let mankind
Reproach thee for a fraud so base.

Neoptolemus

Alas!
What shall I do? Would I were still at Scyros!
For I am most unhappy.

Philoctetes

O my son!
Thou art not base by nature, but misguided
By those who are, to deeds unworthy of thee.
Turn then thy fraud on them who best deserve it;
Restore my arms, and leave me.

Neoptolemus

Speak, my friends,
What's to be done?

[Ulysses enters suddenly.]

Ulysses

Ah! dost thou hesitate?
Traitor, be gone! Give me the arms.

Philoctetes

Ah me!
Ulysses here?

Ulysses

Aye! 'tis Ulysses' self
That stands before thee.

Philoctetes

Then I'm lost, betrayed!
This was the cruel spoiler.

Ulysses

Doubt it not.
'Twas I; I do confess it.

Philoctetes*[to Neoptolemus]*

O my son!
Give me them back.

Ulysses

It must not be; with them
Thyself must go, or we shall drag thee hence.

Philoctetes

And will they force me? O thou daring villain!

Ulysses

They will, unless thou dost consent to go.

Philoctetes

Wilt thou, O Lemnos! wilt thou, mighty Vulcan!
With thy all-conquering fire, permit me thus
To be torn from thee?

Ulysses

Know, great Jove himself
Doth here preside. He hath decreed thy fate;
I but perform his will.

Philoctetes

Detested wretch,
Mak'st thou the gods a cover for thy crime?
Do they teach falsehood?

Ulysses

No, they taught me truth,
And therefore, hence — that way thy journey lies.

40

[Pointing to the sea]

Philoctetes

It doth not.

Ulysses

But I say it must be so.

Philoctetes

And Philoctetes then was born a slave!
I did not know it,

Ulysses

No; I mean to place thee
E'en with the noblest, e'en with those by whom
Proud Troy must perish.

Philoctetes

Never will I go,
Befall what may, whilst this deep cave is open
To bury all my sorrows.

Ulysses

What wouldst do?

Philoctetes

Here throw me down, dash out my desperate brains
Against this rock, and sprinkle it with my blood.

Ulysses *[to the Chorus]*

Seize, and prevent him!

[They seize him.]

Philoctetes

Manacled! O hands!
How helpless are you now! those arms, which once
Protected, thus torn from you! *[To Ulysses]*
Thou abandoned,
Thou shameless wretch! from whom nor truth nor justice,
Naught that becomes the generous mind, can flow,

41

How hast thou used me! how betrayed! Suborned
This stranger, this poor youth, who, worthier far
To be my friend than thine, was only here
Thy instrument; he knew not what he did,
And now, thou seest, repents him of the crime
Which brought such guilt on him, such woes on me.
But thy foul soul, which from its dark recess
Trembling looks forth, beheld him void of art,
Unwilling as he was, instructed him,
And made him soon a master in deceit.
I am thy prisoner now; e'en now thou meanst
To drag me hence, from this unhappy shore,
Where first thy malice left me, a poor exile,
Deserted, friendless, and though living, dead
To all mankind. Perish the vile betrayer!
Oh! I have cursed thee often, but the gods
Will never bear the prayers of Philoctetes.
Life and its joys are thine, whilst I, unhappy,
Am but the scorn of thee, and the Atreidae,
Thy haughty masters. Fraud and force compelled thee,
Or thou hadst never sailed with them to Troy.
I lent my willing aid; with seven brave ships
I ploughed the main to serve them. In return
They cast me forth, disgraced me, left me here.
Thou sayst they did it; they impute the crime
To thee. And what will you do with me now?
And whither must I go? What end, what purpose
Could urge thee to it? I am nothing, lost
And dead already. Wherefore — tell me, wherefore? —
Am I not still the same detested burthen,
Loathsome and lame? Again must Philoctetes
Disturb your holy rites? If I am with you
How can you make libations? That was once
Your vile pretence for inhumanity.
Oh! may you perish for the deed! The gods
Will grant it sure, if justice be their care
And that it is I know. You had not left
Your native soil to seek a wretch like me
Had not some impulse from the powers above,
Spite of yourselves, ordained it. O my country!
And you, O gods! who look upon this deed,
Punish, in pity to me, punish all
The guilty band! Could I behold them perish,
My wounds were nothing; that would heal them all.

Leader[to Ulysses]

Observe, my lord, what bitterness of soul
His words express; he bends not to misfortune,
But seems to brave it.

Ulysses

I could answer him,
Were this a time for words; but now, no more
Than this — I act as best befits our purpose.
Where virtue, truth, and justice are required
Ulysses yields to none; I was not born
To be o'ercome, and yet submit to thee.
Let him remain. Thy arrows shall suffice;
We want thee not! Teucer can draw thy bow
As well as thou; myself with equal strength
Can aim the deadly shaft, with equal skill.
What could thy presence do? Let Lemnos keep thee.
Farewell! perhaps the honours once designed
For thee may be reserved to grace Ulysses.

Philoctetes

Alas! shall Greece then see my deadliest foe
Adorned with arms which I alone should bear?

Ulysses

No more! I must be gone.

Philoctetes[to Neoptolemus]

Son of Achilles,
Thou wilt not leave me too? I must not lose
Thy converse, thy assistance.

Ulysses[to Neoptolemus]

Look not on him;
Away, I charge thee! 'Twould be fatal to us.

Philoctetes[to the Chorus]

Will you forsake me, friends? Dwells no compassion
Within your breasts for me?

Leader[pointing to Neoptolemus]

He is our master;
We speak and act but as his will directs.

Neoptolemus

I know be will upbraid me for this weakness,
But 'tis my nature, and I must consent,
Since Philoctetes asks it. Stay you with him,
Till to the gods our pious prayers we offer,
And all things are prepared for our departure;
Perhaps, meantime, to better thoughts his mind
May turn relenting. We must go. Remember,
When we shall call you, follow instantly.

[Neoptolemus, still with the bow in his hands, goes out with Ulysses. The lines in the following scene between Philoctetes and the Chorus are chanted responsively.]

Philoctetes

O my poor hut! and is it then decreed
Again I come to thee to part no more,
To end my wretched days in this sad cave,
The scene of all my woes? For whither now
Can I betake me? Who will feed, support,
Or cherish Philoctetes? Not a hope
Remains for me. Oh! that th' impetuous storms
Would bear me with them to some distant clime!
For I must perish here.

Chorus

Unhappy man!
Thou hast provoked thy fate; thyself alone
Art to thyself a foe, to scorn the good,
Which wisdom bids thee take, and choose misfortune.

Philoctetes

Wretch that I am, to perish here alone!
Oh! I shall see the face of man no more,
Nor shall my arrows pierce their winged prey,
And bring me sustenance! Such vile delusions
Used to betray me! Oh! that pains like those
I feel might reach the author of my woes!

Chorus

The gods decreed it; we are not to blame.
Heap not thy curses therefore on the guiltless,
But take our friendship.

Philoctetes*[pointing to the sea-shore]*

I behold him there;
E'en now I see him laughing me to scorn
On yonder shore, and in his hands the darts
He waves triumphant, which no arms but these
Had ever borne. O my dear glorious treasure!
Hadst thou a mind to feel th' indignity,
How wouldst thou grieve to change thy noble master,
The friend of great Alcides, for a wretch
So vile, so base, so impious as Ulysses!

Chorus

justice will ever rule the good man's tongue,
Nor from his lips reproach and bitterness
Invidious flow. Ulysses, by the voice
Of Greece appointed, only sought a friend
To join the common cause, and serve his country.

Philoctetes

Hear me, ye winged inhabitants of air,
And you, who on these mountains love to feed,
My savage prey, whom once I could pursue;
Fearful no more of Philoctetes, fly
This hollow rock — I cannot hurt you now;
You need not dread to enter here. Alas!
You now may come, and in your turn regale
On these poor limbs, when I shall be no more.
Where can I hope for food? or who can breathe
This vital air, when life-preserving earth
No longer will assist him?

Chorus

By the gods!
Let me entreat thee, if thou dost regard
Our master, and thy friend, come to him now,
Whilst thou mayst 'scape this sad calamity;

45

Who but thyself would choose to be unhappy
That could prevent it?

Philoctetes

Oh! you have brought back
Once more the sad remembrance of my griefs;
Why, why, my friends, would you afflict me thus?

Chorus

Afflict thee — how?

Philoctetes

Think you I'll e'er return
To hateful Troy?

Chorus

We would advise thee to it.

Philoctetes

I'll hear no more. Go, leave me!

Chorus

That we shall
Most gladly. To the ships, my friends; away! *[Going]*
Obey your orders.

Philoctetes*[stops them]*

By protecting Jove,
Who hears the suppliant's prayer, do not forsake me!

Chorus*[returning]*

Be calm then.

Philoctetes

O my friends! will you then stay?
Do, by the gods I beg you.

Chorus

Why that groan?

Philoctetes

Alas! I die. My wound, my wound! Hereafter
What can I do? You will not leave me! Hear —

Chorus

What canst thou say we do not know already?

Philoctetes

O'erwhelmed by such a storm of griefs as I am,
You should not thus resent a madman's frenzy.

Chorus

Comply then and be happy.

Philoctetes

Never, never!
Be sure of that. Tho' thunder-bearing Jove
Should with his lightnings blast me, would I go?
No! Let Troy perish, perish all the host
Who sent me here to die; but, O my friends!
Grant me this last request.

Chorus

What is it? Speak.

Philoctetes

A sword, a dart, some instrument of death.

Chorus

What wouldst thou do?

Philoctetes

I'd hack off every limb.
Death, my soul longs for death.

Chorus

But wherefore is it?

Philoctetes

I'll seek my father.

Chorus

Whither?

Philoctetes

In the tomb;
There he must be. O Scyros! O my country!
How could I bear to see thee as I am —
I who had left thy sacred shores to aid
The hateful sons of Greece? O misery!

[He goes into the cave.]

Leader of the Chorus*[speaking]*

Ere now we should have taken thee to our ships,
But that advancing this way I behold
Ulysses, and with him Achilles' son.

[Neoptolemus enters still carrying the bow; he is followed closely by Ulysses.]

Ulysses

Why this return? Wherefore this haste?

Neoptolemus

I come
To purge me of my crimes.

Ulysses

Indeed! What crimes?

Neoptolemus

My blind obedience to the Grecian host
And to thy counsels.

Ulysses

Hast thou practised aught
Base or unworthy of thee?

Neoptolemus

Yes; by art
And vile deceit betrayed th' unhappy.

Ulysses

Whom?
Alas! what mean you?

Neoptolemus

Nothing. But the son
Of Poeas —

Ulysses

Ha! what wouldst thou do? My heart
Misgives me.

Neoptolemus

I have ta'en his arms, and now —

Ulysses

Thou wouldst restore them! Speak! Is that thy purpose?
Almighty Jove!

Neoptolemus

Unjustly should I keep
Another's right?

Ulysses

Now, by the gods, thou meanest
To mock me! Dost thou not?

Neoptolemus

If to speak truth
Be mockery.

Ulysses

And does Achilles' son
Say this to me?

Neoptolemus

Why force me to repeat
My words so often to thee?

Ulysses

Once to hear them
Is once indeed too much.

Neoptolemus

Doubt then no more,
For I have told thee all.

Ulysses

There are, remember,
There are who may prevent thee.

Neoptolemus

Who shall dare
To thwart my purpose?

Ulysses

All the Grecian host,
And with them, I.

Neoptolemus

Wise as thou art, Ulysses,
Thou talkst most idly.

Ulysses

Wisdom is not thine
Either in word or deed.

Neoptolemus

Know, to be just
Is better far than to be wise.

Ulysses

But where,
Where is the justice, thus unauthorized,
To give a treasure back thou ow'st to me,
And to my counsels?

Neoptolemus

I have done a wrong,
And I will try to make atonement for it.

Ulysses

Dost thou not fear the power of Greece?

Neoptolemus

I fear
Nor Greece nor thee, when I am doing right.

Ulysses

'Tis not with Troy then we contend. but thee —

Neoptolemus

I know not that.

Ulysses

Seest thou this hand? behold,
It grasps my sword.

Neoptolemus

Mine is alike prepared,
Nor seeks delay.

Ulysses

But I will let thee go;
Greece shall know all thy guilt, and shall revenge it.

[Ulysses departs.]

Neoptolemus

'Twas well determined; always be as wise
As now thou art, and thou mayst live in safety.

[He approaches the cave and calls.]

Ho! son of Poeas! Philoctetes, leave
Thy rocky habitation, and come forth.

Philoctetes *[from the cave]*

What noise was that? Who calls on Philoctetes?

[He comes out.]

Alas! what would you, strangers? Are you come
To heap fresh miseries on me?

Neoptolemus

Be of comfort,
And bear the tidings which I bring.

Philoctetes

I dare not;
Thy flattering tongue hath betrayed me.

Neoptolemus

And is there then no room for penitence?

Philoctetes

Such were thy words, when, seemingly sincere,
Yet meaning ill, thou stolst my arms away.

Neoptolemus

But now it is not so. I only came
To know if thou art resolute to stay,
Or sail with us.

Philoctetes

No more of that; 'tis vain
And useless all.

Neoptolemus

Art thou then fixed?

Philoctetes

I am;
It is impossible to say how firmly.

Neoptolemus

I thought I could have moved thee, but I've done.

Philoctetes

Tis well thou hast; thy labour had been vain;
For never could my soul esteem the man
Who robbed me of my dearest, best possession,
And now would have me listen to his counsels —
Unworthy offspring of the best of men!
Perish th' Atreidae! perish first Ulysses!
Perish thyself!

Neoptolemus

Withhold thy imprecations,
And take thy arrows back.

Philoctetes

A second time
Wouldst thou deceive me?

Neoptolemus

By th' almighty power
Of sacred Jove I swear.

Philoctetes

O joyful sound!
If thou sayst truly.

Neoptolemus

Let my actions speak.
Stretch forth thy hand, and take thy arms again.

[As Neoptolemus gives the bow and arrows to Philoctetes, Ulysses suddenly enters.]

Ulysses

Witness ye gods! Here, in the name of Greece
And the Atreidae, I forbid it.

Philoctetes

Ha!
What voice is that? Ulysses'?

Ulysses

Aye, 'tis I—
I who perforce will carry thee to Troy
Spite of Achilles' son.

Philoctetes

[He aims an arrow directly at Ulysses.]

Not if I aim
This shaft aright.

Neoptolemus*[laying hold of him]*

Now, by the gods, I beg thee
Stop thy rash hand!

Philoctetes

Let go my arm.

Neoptolemus

I will not.

Philoctetes

Shall I not slay my enemy?

Neoptolemus

Oh, no!
'Twould cast dishonour on us both.

[Ulysses hastily departs.]

Philoctetes

Thou knowst,
These Grecian chiefs are loud pretending boasters,
Brave but in tongue, and cowards in the field.

Neoptolemus

I know it; but remember, I restored
Thy arrows to thee, and thou hast no cause
For rage or for complaint against thy friend.

Philoctetes

I own thy goodness. Thou hast shown thyself
Worthy thy birth; no son of Sisyphus,
But of Achilles, who on earth preserved
A fame unspotted, and amongst the dead
Still shines superior, an illustrious shade.

Neoptolemus

Joyful I thank thee for a father's praise,
And for my own; but listen to my words,
And mark me well. Misfortunes, which the gods
Inflict on mortals, they perforce must bear:
But when, oppressed by voluntary woes,
They make themselves unhappy, they deserve not
Our pity or our pardon. Such art thou.
Thy savage soul, impatient of advice,
Rejects the wholesome counsel of thy friend,
And treats him like a foe; but I will speak,
Jove be my witness! Therefore hear my words,
And grave them in thy heart. The dire disease
Thou long hast suffered is from angry heaven,
Which thus afflicts thee for thy rash approach
To the fell serpent, which on Chrysa's shore
Watched o'er the sacred treasures. Know beside,
That whilst the sun in yonder east shall rise,
Or in the west decline, distempered still
Thou ever shalt remain, unless to Troy
Thy willing mind transport thee. There the sons
Of Aesculapius shall restore thee — there
By my assistance shalt thou conquer Troy.
I know it well; for that prophetic sage,
The Trojan captive Helenus, foretold
It should be so. "Proud Troy (he added then)
This very year must fall; if not, my life
Shall answer for the falsehood." Therefore yield.
Thus to be deemed the first of Grecians, thus
By Poeas' favourite sons to be restored,
And thus marked out the conqueror of Troy,
Is sure distinguished happiness.

Philoctetes

O life!
Detested, why wilt thou still keep me here?

55

Why not dismiss me to the tomb! Alas!
What can I do? How can I disbelieve
My generous friend? I must consent, and yet
Can I do this, and look upon the sun?
Can I behold my friends — will they forgive,
Will they associate with me after this?
And you, ye heavenly orbs that roll around me,
How will ye bear to see me linked with those
Who have destroyed me, e'en the sons of Atreus,
E'en with Ulysses, source of all my woes?
My sufferings past I could forget; but oh!
I dread the woes to come; for well I know
When once the mind's corrupted it brings forth
Unnumbered crimes, and ills to ills succeed.
It moves my wonder much that thou, my friend,
Shouldst thus advise me, whom it ill becomes
To think of Troy. I rather had believed
Thou wouldst have sent me far, far off from those
Who have defrauded thee of thy just right,
And gave thy arms away. Are these the men
Whom thou wouldst serve? whom thou wouldst thus compel me
To save and to defend? It must not be.
Remember, O my son! the solemn oath
Thou gav'st to bear me to my native soil.
Do this, my friend, remain thyself at Scyros,
And leave these wretches to be wretched still.
Thus shalt thou merit double thanks, from me
And from thy father; nor by succour given
To vile betrayers prove thyself as vile.

Neoptolemus

Thou sayst most truly. Yet confide in heaven,
Trust to thy friend, and leave this hated place.

Philoctetes

Leave it! For whom? For Troy and the Atreidae?
These wounds forbid it.

Neoptolemus

They shall all be healed,
Where I will carry thee.

Philoctetes

An idle tale
Thou tellst me. surely; dost thou not?

Neoptolemus

I speak
What best may serve us both.

Philoctetes

But, speaking thus,
Dost thou not fear the' offended gods?

Neoptolemus

Why fear them?
Can I offend the gods by doing good?

Philoctetes

What good? To whom? To me or to the' Atreidae?

Neoptolemus

I am thy friend, and therefore would persuade thee.

Philoctetes

And therefore give me to my foes.

Neoptolemus

Alas!
Let not misfortunes thus transport thy soul
To rage and bitterness.

Philoctetes

Thou wouldst destroy me.

Neoptolemus

Thou knowst me not.

Philoctetes

I know th' Atreidae well,
Who left me here.

Neoptolemus

They did; yet they perhaps,
E'en they, O Philoctetes! may preserve thee.

Philoctetes

I never will to Troy.

Neoptolemus

What's to be done?
Since I can ne'er persuade thee, I submit;
Live on in misery.

Philoctetes

Then let me suffer;
Suffer I must; but, oh! perform thy promise;
Think on thy plighted faith, and guard me home
Instant, my friend, nor ever call back Troy
To my remembrance; I have felt enough
From Troy already.

Neoptolemus

Let us go; prepare!

Philoctetes

O glorious sound!

Neoptolemus

Bear thyself up.

Philoctetes

I will,
If possible.

Neoptolemus

But how shall I escape
The wrath of Greece?

Philoctetes

Oh! think not of it.

Neoptolemus

What
If they should waste my kingdom?

Philoctetes

I'll be there.

Neoptolemus

Alas! what canst thou do?

Philoctetes

And with these arrows
Of my Alcides —

Neoptolemus

Ha! What sayst thou?

Philoctetes

Drive
Thy foes before me. Not a Greek shall dare
Approach thy borders.

Neoptolemus

If thou wilt do this,
Salute the earth, and instant hence. Away!

[Hercules appears from above, and speaks as he moves forward.]

Hercules

Stay, son of Poeas! Lo to thee 'tis given
Once more to see and hear thy loved Alcides,
Who for thy sake hath left yon heavenly mansions,
And comes to tell thee the decrees of Jove;
To turn thee from the paths thou meanst to tread,
And guide thy footsteps right. Therefore attend.
Thou knowst what toils, what labours I endured,
Ere I by virtue gained immortal fame;
Thou too like me by toils must rise to glory —
Thou too must suffer, ere thou canst be happy;
Hence with thy friend to Troy, where honour calls,
Where health awaits thee — where, by virtue raised

59

To highest rank, and leader of the war,
Paris, its hateful author, shalt thou slay,
Lay waste proud Troy, and send thy trophies home,
Thy valour's due reward, to glad thy sire
On Oeta's top. The gifts which Greece bestows
Must thou reserve to grace my funeral pile,
And be a monument to after-ages
Of these all-conquering arms. Son of Achilles

[Turning to Neoptolemus]

(For now to thee I speak), remember this,
Without his aid thou canst not conquer Troy,
Nor Philoctetes without thee succeed;
Go then, and, like two lions in the field
Roaming for prey, guard ye each other well;
My Aesculapius will I send e'en now
To heal thy wounds — Then go, and conquer Troy;
But when you lay the vanquished city waste.
Be careful that you venerate the gods;
For far above all other gifts doth Jove,
Th' almighty father, hold true piety:
Whether we live or die, that still survives
Beyond the reach of fate, and is immortal.

Philoctetes*[chanting]*

Once more to let me hear that wished-for voice,
To see thee after so long time, was bliss
I could not hope for. Oh! I will obey
Thy great commands most willingly.

Neoptolemus*[chanting]*

And I.

Hercules*[chanting]*

Delay not then. For lo! a prosperous wind
Swells in thy sail. The time invites. Adieu!

[Hercules disappears above.]

Philoctetes*[chanting]*

I will but pay my salutations here,
And instantly depart. To thee, my cave,
Where I so long have dwelt, I bid farewell!

And you, ye nymphs, who on the watery plains
Deign to reside, farewell! Farewell the noise
Of beating waves, which I so oft have heard
From the rough sea, which by the black winds driven
O'erwhelmed me, shivering. Oft th' Hermaean mount
Echoed my plaintive voice, by wintry storms
Afflicted, and returned me groan for groan.
Now, ye fresh fountains, each Lycaean spring,
I leave you now. Alas! I little thought
To leave you ever. And thou sea-girt isle,
Lemnos, farewell! Permit me to depart
By thee unblamed, and with a prosperous gale
To go where fate demands, where kindest friends
By counsel urge me, where all-powerful Jove
In his unerring wisdom hath decreed.

Chorus*[chanting]*

Let us be gone, and to the ocean nymphs
Our humble prayers prefer, that they would all
Propitious smile, and grant us safe return.

Printed in Great Britain
by Amazon

57943036R00038